FOURTH-GRADE CELEBRITY

"Dear Cassandra Eleanor..."

FOURTH-GRADE CELEBRITY

PATRICIA REILLY GIFF

Illustrated by Leslie Morrill

A YEARLING BOOK

Published by
Dell Publishing
a division of
Bantam Doubleday Dell Publishing Group, Inc.
666 Fifth Avenue
New York, New York 10103

ISBN: 0-440-42676-6

Reprinted by arrangement with Delacorte Press

Printed in the United States of America

One Previous Edition

September 1989

10 9 8 7 6 5 4 3 2

CW

FOR
200TH STREET
AND THE PEOPLE
WHO STILL LIVE THERE
IN MY MIND,
ESPECIALLY
MY MOTHER AND FATHER
AND ANNIE

1

"Darlene Verona is a stinky, rotten thing for not inviting me to her birthday party," Casey said. She puffed out her cheeks and blew through her braces. "But if I were Darlene, I wouldn't invite me either."

Walter didn't answer.

"Hey, are you still there?" She peered through the Cyclone fence into the Secret Passageway, a space that ran in between the yards on 200th Street and the Ogden Schoolyard. It was a narrow alley filled with weeds and rocks and candy wrappers that the kids were always poking through the fence.

It was getting so dark, Casey could just about see Walter's green sweater. He was down on his hands and knees, looking into a hole he had dug in the center of the Passageway.

"I can't find them," he said finally. He pushed his

glasses higher on his nose. "I think they've disappeared."

Casey snorted. "Dead fish can't walk away. Keep looking."

Walter grunted.

She sat down on the grass, holding the book they kept for their science experiments, and leaned against the fence. "I know why Darlene didn't invite me. I have no zip. No style. I'm a lump of vanilla pudding."

"Nothing wrong with vanilla pudding. It's my favorite kind."

"Nothing wrong!" she said, her voice rising. "Nobody notices me. The school year is two weeks old and Mrs. Petty still calls me Vanessa. It's always my sister Van. Van is prettier. Van is smarter. Actually, what Van is is a pain in the A."

Walter looked up. "What brought this on all of a sudden?"

"Listen, Walt, all my life Van's been the perfect Valentine. It never bothered me that much before, but I've been thinking about it lately." She made a face. "Mrs. Petty made me bring home yesterday's work to be signed because it was kind of a mess. My mother carried on for ten minutes. All I heard about was my sister Van. How good she is in school—how terrific." She ran her tongue across her braces. "How disgusting."

Walter stopped digging. "I found them. I can see the corner of the can sticking out." He dug up a bright red coffee can and pried off the lid. "We shouldn't have started this so late. It's hard to get a good look at them."

"Do you want me to get a flashlight?"

"No, I guess they're about the same as they were last week." He poked his hand into the can. "Skin is still on them. Mark down 'no change' in the book."

"Good idea," she said. "We'll start earlier next week. And remember, it's my turn to check them out."

Walter pushed the can back into the hole and began to drop dirt in on top of it.

"Walt?" Casey said. "How about nominating me for class president?"

"I would, Casey," he said, brushing the dirt off his hands, "but I've already promised George Pomeroy I'd vote for him."

"I'll worry about that when we get to the voting part. How about it? I'll give you all my last year's baseball cards."

"Worthless."

"How about this year's?"

Walter climbed the fence and landed on her side with a thud.

"Look," she said. She squinted up at him, trying to see better in the dark. "I'm going to make myself over. Become a celebrity or something. But I need a little cooperation. By the end of this year I want everyone in school to know my name. At least. Let them know that Van isn't the only Valentine in school."

He stood there considering. "Get Tracy Matson off my back."

"Who?"

"Some idiot girl." He stopped to trim his thumbnail with his teeth. "She lived in the town where we stayed for a week on vacation last summer. Every time she sends me a letter, my mother makes me write back."

"And you'll nominate me tomorrow?"

Casey ran her tongue over her braces. "How can I—"

"Simple. She's just looking for a pen pal. Write and tell her you're a friend of mine. Say I can't write anymore, that my hand dropped off or something."

"And you'll nominate me tomorrow?"

"It's a deal. Walk me back to my house and I'll give you her address."

Casey stood up and dusted off the seat of her pants. "Let's go, Walter. Things are looking up already. A new pen pal and a nomination for class president practically in my pocket."

2

Dear Tracy Matson,

My name is Casey Valentine. I used to be Walter Moles's best friend. I know you will be sorry to learn that Walter passed on last night. He died heroically after capturing two kidnappers who were after me. (I'm rich.) I am having a gold medal made for his parents out of my allowance. ($500 per week.)

It's a shame that this happened now. We were conducting important experiments for the government (to see what happens to fish after they've been buried for a while).

Please do not write to Walter anymore. And don't write to his family. They want to forget about the whole thing. Write to me instead.

Your new friend,
Cassandra Eleanor Valentine

P.S. Before he died, Walter nominated me for class president.

3

Casey crammed the last of the apple pie into her mouth, washed most of it down with a gulp of milk, and rubbed the napkin across her face.

"May I be excused?" she asked her mother and scraped back the kitchen chair.

"Tell Van it's her night to do the dishes."

"With pleasure."

"And, Casey . . ."

She waited on one foot.

"Push the hair out of your eyes."

She gave her bangs a quick swipe with her hand and took the stairs to the bedroom two at a time. "Are you in there, Van?"

Her older sister was standing on tiptoe on the footboard of her bed, balancing herself with her fingertips on the ceiling.

7

"Mother said—" Casey began.

"Shut up a minute, will you, Casey? How am I ever going to get to be an Olympic gymnast with all these interruptions?"

Casey watched Van inch her way across the footboard. Her sister was a great athlete, even though there were fingerprints all over the ceiling. She was the smartest kid in sixth grade, too. There was no doubt about it. Van was a genius.

"It's your night to do the dishes," Casey said as Van reached the end of the footboard.

"It's always my night to do the dishes." Van did a flip off the edge of the footboard, landed upright, then stood on her head.

"Why do you have to do that all the time?" Casey asked.

"Keeping fit," Van answered, smoothing her short blond hair.

Casey flopped across her own bed. "I'll do you a little favor and do the dishes tonight if you want."

"What do I have to do?"

"Write a limerick for me."

"Are you kidding? I thought you were going to be a writer when you grow up."

"A sensible writer—mystery stories, stuff like that," Casey said. "But I have to have a limerick for Monday. All I can think of is 'There was an old man from—'"

"That's a good start."

"Come on, Vanny."

"Sorry, Casey, I just finished my own homework and I'm not much good at those things. You're the one with imagination."

Van stood on her head.

"Please?"

Van cocked her head to one side. "You look like a schnauzer with your hair hanging over your eyes like that."

Casey blew her hair off her forehead. "Can't help it. I'm trying to get it to grow long like Darlene's." She glanced in the mirror and dragged her bangs back as hard as she could. "See, they just won't stay." She turned around so Van could watch her brown hair pop back over her forehead.

"I don't know why you want to get rid of your bangs, anyway."

"Nobody in my class wears bangs anymore."

"I don't want to hurt your feelings, but I think you look better with bangs. Hides some of your freckles. Makes your face a little prettier."

Casey looked back at the mirror. Her face was long, and skinny like the rest of her. Not nearly as pretty as Darlene's. She turned and stuck her tongue out at Van, feeling hurt. "You don't look so hot either, Van. You're starting to get pimples. You'll probably have a face like a pan of worms by next year."

Van made a face and picked a banana peel off the radio. "I'm not going to clean this mess of a room again." She tossed the peel into the wastebasket. "What a slob you are, Casey. I wish I could move up to the attic and room by myself."

"I wish you could too," Casey said to her sister's back as Van went downstairs to do the dishes.

Casey wandered over to her closet, grabbed a pile of clothes, and draped them on her bed.

Look, she said to herself, you'd better wear something a little special tomorrow. She held a pair of tan pants in front of her and glanced in the mirror. "Look like a camel," she muttered and dropped them on the floor. She picked up her blue-plaid pants and scratched at a powdery white stain that covered one knee. Most of it came off, but there was still a grayish spot underneath.

She spit on it and rubbed a little harder. She'd have to wait and see it when it dried. She hung it over her pink lamp shade and tried to decide on something else, just in case.

The trouble was that everything was a little spotty or a little ripped. She couldn't understand it. Two weeks ago, before school started, her mother had taken her to Susan's Discount Shop for a bunch of new stuff. Now everything was a mess. And these clothes weren't nearly as great as the cashier lady had said they were. No one in the class seemed to be wearing pastel shirts and plaid pants.

She left the clothes in a pile on the bed. Carry a pocketbook, she advised herself, and hold it right over the stain on the blue slacks. No one will ever notice.

She looked doubtfully at the stain, then walked over to Van's closet. Locked again. She wiggled the knob.

She tiptoed to the top of the stairs and leaned over. Van was doing the dishes. She could hear her talking with Mom.

Grinning, she sped back into the bedroom and began to search. She looked under Van's mattress, in her jewelry box, and under the lamp on her night table.

Finally she stood in the center of the room and twirled around slowly. "Where is that key?" she whispered. She turned around again and pounced on the wastebasket in the corner. Bending over, she lifted it until she saw the silver gleam of the key.

"Aha, foolish Van," she said, twisting an imaginary mustache. "Nevair can you fool zee great Inspector Valentine." Smiling, she rolled her tongue over her braces. If that stain didn't fade out a little, she'd borrow something of Van's.

One problem solved. Then she frowned. There was still the limerick gnawing at her. "There was an old man named—" She sat cross-legged in the middle of Van's bed. "There was a young man—"

It was a shame she had to waste her time on such a ratty assignment. There was an important list she wanted to make and a book she wanted to finish. The book was a great mystery, and she was sure she knew who had hidden the letter in the old trunk. She just had to find out if she was right. She picked up the book and began to read.

An hour later Van was back. "Do you have to peel your nail polish off all over the bed?" she said. "And why do you have to lie on my bed all the time, anyway?"

Casey looked up guiltily. "Too much junk on mine. Besides, I meant to lie here and read for only a few minutes. What time is it?"

"Nine thirty."

Casey slammed the book shut and stood up. "Darn. I have to wash my hair."

"Mother said to get ready for bed."

"I'll hurry. I have to look good tomorrow. Mrs. Petty

is going to announce the results of the election for class president. And I'm one of the candidates."

"You?"

"Yes, me."

"Hey, that's pretty good. I hope you win. Who nominated you?"

Casey scraped some more Blue Torch nail polish off her thumb. "Walter."

"How did you get him to do that?"

"None of your business."

Van shrugged and picked up the blue-plaid pants. "What's this filthy thing doing on the lamp?"

"Is it? Filthy, I mean?"

"Look at this big stain."

"Vanny, how about doing me a little favor?"

Van glanced at her closet door. "Don't you dare touch any of my clothes."

"The closet's locked. How can I?" she asked, carefully keeping her eyes away from the wastebasket.

"And it's going to stay locked too," Van said emphatically, "or my closet will be a wreck just like yours. Do you know I saw an old dried-up liverwurst sandwich on your closet floor before?"

Casey grabbed her pajamas from under her pillow and went down the hall to the bathroom, muttering, "There was a young lady from—"

It wasn't until she was back in bed, thinking about the liverwurst sandwich and trying to remember when she'd left it there, that she realized Van had been in her closet.

"Hey. Why were you—" she began, leaning up on one elbow, but Van was sound asleep.

13

4

WAYS TO BECOME A CELEBRITY

BY

CASSANDRA ELEANOR VALENTINE

1. Become class president.
2. Rescue child, cat, dog, etc., from burning building.
3. Do something different, unusual, like speaking French.
4. Become an athlete. Do 100 pull-ups on W.M.'s bar in garage.
5. Get name in paper.

Ways to become a celebrity.

5

The next morning Casey chewed each mouthful of cereal ten times and spread three coats of Blue Torch polish on her nails. Finally Van left for school without her.

Fifteen minutes later Casey skipped out of the house dressed in Van's green corduroy jumper and ice-blue shirt. Cutting across Walter's lawn next door to get to the Ogden School gate, she reflected that it was pretty convenient living only two houses away from the entrance to the school. The bell had rung, but she caught the line into her class before it reached the second floor.

She cut in ahead of Gunther Reed.

"Think you're going to win today?" he asked.

Ordinarily she didn't speak to him, but today she smiled. "I hope so."

"Acting pretty friendly all of a sudden," he said. "Think I'm going to vote for you?"

"Don't bother," she said and turned her back on him.

She sat down at her table and arranged Van's jumper carefully underneath her so it wouldn't wrinkle. Then she rooted around in her drawer for a pencil and a piece of paper.

She smoothed the edge of the paper and wrote in her best handwriting:

A LIMERICK

BY

CASSANDRA ELEANOR VALENTINE

She saw a shadow on her paper and looked up. Mrs. Petty stood there watching her. Her round face was reddish and her front teeth, slightly separated, rested on her lower lip.

"That's homework, Van—er—Cassandra," she said, spraying slightly as she said the *s*'s.

Casey nodded and put the limerick paper away. She looked at the blackboard. Four jobs to do this morning, she calculated. Arithmetic, social studies, science, and art.

She took out her math book. Leafing through, she found page 27. She sighed. It was the worst: long division. Not because she didn't know how to do it. She did. In fact, sometimes it was interesting to estimate all over the place and finally come up with something close. The trouble was that there were so many chances to make mistakes because of all that multiplying and subtracting.

She ripped a page out of her loose-leaf notebook and began to divide. She worked as fast as she could because she was in a hurry to get to the social studies assignment. She was supposed to pretend she had traveled across the prairie in a covered wagon and was writing to a friend back East to tell about her adventures. It was the kind of assignment she loved. She intended to put in lots of danger, with hostile Indians kidnapping her and wild beasts chasing her every step of the way to California.

She worked her way through the morning, stopping occasionally to think about the class election. If she won, she'd consider it a sign that her whole life would change. Everybody would stop thinking Van was so perfect and start to realize that she, Casey, was pretty important too.

Finally she took out the page she had labeled for her limerick, thought for a moment, then scribbled something down that almost rhymed:

> There once were two Valentine girls.
> The oldest one seemed like a pearl.
> She could stand on her head
> At the foot of the bed,
> But she wasn't so hot after all.

Then she sat back and sucked air through her braces to make a swishing noise while she waited for Mrs. Petty to announce the winner of the fourth-grade election for class president.

It seemed to take forever. Not that she thought she had much chance of winning. In fact, she probably had no chance at all. She knew of only two people in the class who had voted for her—Mindy Gregory, who was another blob of vanilla pudding, and Casey herself. And she really wasn't so sure about Mindy's vote. Lately Mindy had done a lot of smiling at George Pomeroy, and since he was running, too . . .

Suddenly she stopped swishing. Suppose Mindy hadn't voted for her? And suppose no one else had voted for her? Even though she had disguised her handwriting carefully, making big wavery letters uphill across the page, it would be pretty obvious to the whole class that she had voted for herself.

Mrs. Petty rapped a plump hand on the edge of the desk. She stood there fiddling with the large white beads she always wore.

"Boys and girls," she said finally, "if everyone is finished with his boardwork, we'll discuss the class election now. I've just finished counting the votes."

Casey swished gently and looked out the window as if she weren't particularly interested in the results.

"We have a problem with this election," Mrs. Petty said. "The winner was Catherine Wilson. But Catherine will be out of school for the next few weeks with a broken leg, so we really can't wait for her to come back. We need a president now."

Casey looked back at her with interest. Maybe she had a chance.

Mrs. Petty twisted her beads. "The runner-up was George Pomeroy."

Casey shot an accusing look at Mindy's back, two seats in front of her.

"But," Mrs. Petty said, "Mrs. Pomeroy called this

morning. Unfortunately, the Pomeroys are moving very shortly. . . ." She broke off and smiled at George. "We'll really miss you. However," she continued, "we still need a class president. The only candidate left is Cassandra Valentine."

Casey swished once in pure joy.

"No fair," Gunther yelled from the back of the room.

Mrs. Petty looked at him. "That will do, Gunther."

"She probably had only one vote." He snickered. "Her own."

Darlene Verona raised her hand. "How many votes did Casey have, anyway?" she asked.

Mrs. Petty hesitated.

Casey sank down in her seat. Gunther was probably right, she thought bitterly.

"Maybe we should start over, pull a name out of a hat or something," Darlene went on. "I'm not sure Casey is really the people's choice, anyway."

"Right," someone in the back of the room said.

Mrs. Petty clapped her hands. "Well—maybe that's what we should do. Yes. We'll put everyone's name in a box and choose the class president that way. We'll have to hurry, though—it's almost lunchtime."

Casey was so disappointed she could hardly tear a little piece of paper out of her assignment pad to write her name for the box. Slowly she sharpened her pencil in her rocket sharpener.

With her pencil, not even bothering to disguise her handwriting, she wrote in big letters: CASSANDRA VALENTINE. She folded the paper carefully in half and dropped it into the box Mrs. Petty was passing around the room.

She folded the paper and dropped it into the box.

6

Twenty minutes later, in the cafeteria, Casey slid her tray along the rack with one hand and fished for her lunch ticket with the other.

"Just a minute," she told Betty, the cook. "It's in my wallet somewhere."

Betty wiped her hand across her forehead. "Fourth time you've lost your ticket in two weeks."

Behind Casey a six-grader groaned. "Hurry up, will you? By the time I get off this line, lunch will be over."

"Wait a minute," Casey said over her shoulder. "Doing the best I can."

She dug deeper into the zippered compartment of her wallet and held up a wrinkled blue lunch ticket. "Told you it was here." She dropped it on the counter and slid some change on top of it.

"Think I'll treat myself to an extra hot dog." She smiled at the cook. "It's a special day."

"Birthday?"

Casey shook her head. "No. I was elected class president this morning."

Someone in the back of the line groaned again. "Come on. Move."

Betty plunked the hot dogs on the tray. Casey picked it up and went to one of the fourth-grade tables. For a moment she stood there uncertainly. Today she had been last in her class line. She hated it when that happened. It meant that all the kids were seated ahead of her, hunched over their sandwiches, talking to each other. No one would pay attention to her standing there or move over for her to sit down.

"Any room here?" she asked, squeezing on the end next to Mindy Gregory. She nodded to Walter, who was at the other end of the table, leaning against the wall.

"Bought myself two hot dogs today in honor of the occasion," she told Mindy.

"What occasion?" Mindy asked through her milk straw.

"Being elected class president. Did you forget already?"

Gunther Reed, on the other side of the table, looked at Casey and hooted. "I wouldn't call having your name picked out of a box being elected."

"Shut up, Goony," Casey answered. She took a huge bite of her hot dog. This had been some morning. By the time Mrs. Petty had chosen George Pomeroy to pull a name out of the box, Casey had almost given

23

up. She held her breath while George gave the paper he had picked to the teacher.

Mrs. Petty unfolded the paper so slowly it seemed to take an hour.

Finally she looked directly at Casey. "Well, well," she said. "It's Van—I mean, Cassandra Valentine."

"Me!" Casey said.

"What do you mean—me?" Mindy asked in a loud voice.

Casey jumped. She had almost forgotten she was in the cafeteria, eating her lunch.

"Sorry, Mindy. I guess I was daydreaming. Thinking of being elected—I mean, picked out of the box."

Gunther made a rude noise. "I suppose this is all we're going to hear about through the whole lunch hour."

"Shut up, Goony," Casey and Mindy said together.

Encouraged because this was the first time anyone had stuck up for her against Gunther, Casey grinned at Mindy. "Maybe you can help me this year," she said. "You could be sort of a deputy or something."

"Luuuck-y," Gunther said, drawing the word out.

"Why do you have to sit here all the time, Goony, when you're such a pest?" Casey asked.

"I was here first," he said. "Remember? Half of your behind is still in the aisle."

"What took you so long to get down to lunch today, anyway?" Mindy asked.

"Mrs. Petty wanted to see me."

"About what?"

"About being class president. She said I'd have to be a model now."

Gunther made a face. "Some model you are, Tinsel Teeth."

Casey blushed. "I can't help wearing braces. Besides, Mrs. Petty meant a model of good behavior, not a model like in the magazines."

"Good thing." He snorted and swung his legs over the bench, overhanded the remains of his lunch into the wastebasket, and disappeared out the door leading to the schoolyard.

"Don't pay any attention to him, Casey," Mindy said. She looked at Casey critically. "When those braces come off, your teeth will probably look as good as everybody else's."

Casey winced and ran her tongue across the top of her hot dog. "Why does school mustard always taste so yucky?"

Mindy shrugged. She seemed more interested in listening to Darlene Verona on her other side tell about how great her birthday party was going to be.

Casey pretended she couldn't hear. Anyway, she was relieved that Mindy hadn't asked what else Mrs. Petty had said. She really didn't want anyone to know, except maybe Walter, who always listened and never had much to say.

Just before lunch Mrs. Petty had crooked her finger at Casey, and as the rest of the class started to file out of the room to the cafeteria, she motioned for Casey to sit on the chair next to her desk.

"Well, Van," she said, smiling, "you got to be president, after all."

"Casey."

"Yes indeed, Cassandra. You'll have some big responsibilities this year. I hope you're up to them."

Casey lowered her head. Mrs. Petty was spraying the desk lightly with *s*'s as she talked.

"I think you'll make a good leader," Mrs. Petty continued, "that is, if you can pull yourself together. Some of your ideas are a little . . ." She paused and looked up at the ceiling. "A little peculiar."

If only Mrs. Petty could learn to speak without using the letter *s* so often, Casey thought. Or maybe she could work it out so she wouldn't have to say it at all. She could call children with *s* in their names "dear," and say things like "want" instead of "wish." Too bad the principal's name was Mr. Rosenstrauss. She really couldn't call him "dear. . . ."

"Cassandra," Mrs. Petty said sharply.

Casey jumped. "Yes, Mrs. Petty."

"Do you understand?"

Casey tried to remember what Mrs. Petty had just said. By the look of the desk, whatever it was must have had plenty of *s*'s in it. Finally she gave up. "Be neater?"

"What I'm saying, Cassandra, is that you have to be a model for the rest of the twenty-two people in this room. Be more—well, more like your sister Van."

Casey gritted her teeth.

Mrs. Petty fiddled with her beads. "Well, you'll be late for lunch. Do the best you can this year."

Casey stood up.

"And do try to be a little neater, dear. A good president is careful, remember?"

Casey had nodded one last time and sped out the door toward the lunchroom.

"Hey, Casey," Mindy said, "you've been dreaming this whole lunch hour. Pay attention."

Casey picked up her other hot dog and started to eat. She ducked as she saw her sister Van go by with her best friend, Sue Verona, Darlene's older sister.

Then her eyes widened. Van, that weasel, was carrying Casey's canvas pocketbook. So that's what Van had been doing in her closet when she found the liverwurst sandwich.

Casey stood up. But then she remembered she was wearing Van's jumper. She wiped a little mustard off the front of it and sat down again.

Darlene leaned across Mindy. "Your sister Van got to be president of her class, too."

"How do you know?"

"Met my sister Susan in the girls' room. She said that practically everyone in the class voted for Van."

Casey pushed the last of her hot dog into her mouth and stood up, chewing. "I guess we can go outside until the bell rings," she said as soon as she could talk.

7

Friday after school Casey took the back steps two at a time, nudged the door open, and dropped her books in the kitchen. She reached for the largest apple in the bowl on the table, but switched to a smaller one when she noticed a brown spot on the bottom. Probably full of worms, she thought. Leave it for Van.

She sniffed. What was that smell? She walked into the hall and peered into the living room. Cans of paint and drop cloths all over the place. It looked as if the whole house would be in a mess for days.

Her mother sat on the couch staring at little cards of different colors.

Casey leaned over her. "What are they?"

"Paint samples," her mother answered. "We're going

"What are they?" Casey asked.

to do the living room in beige." She held a gray card up in the air and squinted at it. "Can't decide on a color for the hall, though."

"Pretty dull, if you ask me," Casey said.

Her father appeared in the doorway. "What do you want, Casey? Polka dots?"

Casey looked up at him and giggled. "Aren't you home from work early?"

"I had some extra time off coming," he answered, "so I thought I'd get a start on the painting. You and Van better get together and decide on a color for your room."

Casey stood there considering. "Why does it have to be one color?" she said thoughtfully. "Maybe we should do it in wide stripes. We could use the Olympic colors—you know, a stripe of blue, yellow, black, then a stripe of green, red."

"Leave it to you, Casey," said Van from the hall. "Who ever heard of all those colors in one room? I vote for a pale blue."

"No one around here has any imagination at all," Casey grumbled.

"I might have a tough time painting all those stripes anyway, Casey," her father said, grinning. "You have a couple of days to decide, girls. I'm going to do the living room first."

Casey shrugged. "I'm going out then. We'll talk about it later." She stood up and wandered out to the kitchen. On the counter was a pink envelope. It was a letter from Tracy Matson. Casey folded it in half and tucked it in her pocket.

A minute later she climbed the fence to the Secret Passageway, pausing to yell for Walter over her shoulder. Then she settled herself on a pile of leaves and leaned back against the fence.

She looked up to see Walter loping down the driveway.

"Hi, Prez," he said as he vaulted the fence. "So you got to be a celebrity, after all."

"Between you and me, things were pretty close there for a while." She looked through the fence into the schoolyard, where Gunther was riding his bicycle, and frowned. "Mostly because of that rat, Goony Reed. But I shouldn't complain—I probably got only one vote anyway. Then I got in by the skin of my teeth, picked out of a box, as Goony said. But good old Van had about a thousand people voting for her." She sucked on her braces in annoyance.

"I voted for you."

"Are you kidding, Walt?" she asked, immediately cheering up. She took a bite out of her apple and held the other side up to him.

He shook his head.

"Go on, it's good." She wiped her mouth with the back of her hand. "So I got to be president, but there's a lot more to being a celebrity than this. I told you, I want everybody in the school to know my name, instead of saying, 'That's Van Valentine's little sister,' all the time. But it's going to take some figuring to see how I'm going to manage . . ." She broke off. "Are you listening to me?"

"Trying to see if I can set these leaves on fire." He held up a magnifying glass. "Get the sun to shine through in the right way and—"

"And the next thing you know," she cut in, "you'll burn down the whole neighborhood. Hey, I almost forgot, more good news."

He looked up.

"I have here," she said, reaching into her pocket, "my very first letter from my very first pen pal."

"Big deal, Lucille."

"Very funny. Let me see what she has to say." She tore open the envelope and lowered her head over the letter. Then she looked up. "Good grief. Wait till you see the mess we're in now. It's a good thing my mother doesn't read my mail. She'd kill me."

He leaned over and took the letter out of her hands.

Dear Cassandra Eleanor:

Thank you for writting to me. I hope you write more often then Walter did.

I'm sorry to hear about Walter. Did they shoot him, or what? My mother is going to write a letter to Mrs. Moles to tell her she feels terruble or she may even send flowers.

I am in the 4th grade in the Thaddeus Lowell School. I'm a grate swimmer and I'm the best fisherman in the town of High Flats.

How are you? I hope you are fine. I am so glad that you are writting to me. I never had a rich fiend before. I've told everyone in my class about you and they are waiting to read your letters.

I guess a rich kid like you has a lot of things to do.
I have a lot of things to do too.

Write soon.

> Your fiend,
> Tracy

P.S. I hope you were elected class president.

Walter trimmed the edge of his thumbnail with his
teeth. "Kid can't spell too well."

"What are we going to do?" Casey asked.

"I think we should have told her my hand dropped
off."

"Ha, ha," Casey answered. She picked up a pebble
and threw it through a hole in the Cyclone fence.
"Maybe we could send another letter. Tell her the
whole town has the plague. People are dying off like
flies, and your parents were buried last—"

"Listen, Casey, the florist's truck could pull up at
my door any minute. Remember, Tracy must have
written this letter a couple of days ago." He checked
the postmark on the envelope. "I told you that girl is
nothing but a pest."

For a moment there was silence. Casey picked up a
stick and started a ticktacktoe in the dirt. "Maybe we'd
better go sit on your front steps," she said finally.

He stood up. "Right. We'll wait for the florist and
wave him off or something."

Together they hopped the fence and started down
the driveway.

Mrs. Moles was standing at her back door. "Where
have you been?" she asked Walter. "I've been calling

for the last ten minutes. It's time to eat." She turned to Casey. "Pancakes and sausages for supper. Want to stay?"

Casey hesitated, weighing the pancakes, which she loved, against going home and trying to forget about the florist and what would happen when he arrived at the Moleses' house.

"Er . . ." she said at last, deciding in favor of the pancakes, "I'll stay."

Mrs. Moles laughed. "It doesn't sound as if you're wildly enthusiastic."

Casey felt her cheeks redden. "I didn't mean—"

"Just teasing," Mrs. Moles said. "Run and tell your mother."

Five minutes later Casey stood in the Moles kitchen, scooping knives and forks out of the drawer while Walter fed his cat, Carrots.

"We'll set the dining-room table tonight," Mrs. Moles said.

Casey stopped scooping. "Someone's birthday?"

"No, Walter's grandmother is staying with us for a few days. And"—she stopped to check the sausages sizzling on the stove—"I received a beautiful little bouquet of flowers today. It looks too pretty for the kitchen. Go take a look."

Casey laid the silverware gently on the counter and went into the dining room. In the middle of the table was a small bowl of yellow daisies.

Mrs. Moles's voice trailed after her. ". . . a lovely thing to do. But I can't understand—hardly know the people."

Casey leaned back against the wall and gulped. "Beautiful," she said, "just beautiful."

At dinner Walter sat across the table from her. Every time Casey looked at him she wondered if he felt as guilty as she did. Walter's grandmother, Mrs. Thorrien, kept saying how lovely the daisies were, and Mrs. Moles kept wondering why Mrs. Matson would want to send them flowers.

"There was no message on the card," Mrs. Moles said, shaking her head. "It was simply signed Janet and Robert Matson."

"Bunch of nuts, if you ask me," Walter said.

Casey felt a giggle coming and quickly turned to Mrs. Thorrien. "Do you think you could teach me some words?"

Mrs. Thorrien looked at her over her glasses. "I am," she said, "hard of hearing. Did you say words?"

"Yes."

"Words." Mrs. Thorrien nodded. "What kind?"

"Any kind."

"Mother," Mrs. Moles yelled, "I think Casey means in French."

"Oh." Mrs. Thorrien nodded again. "I understand now. *Mais oui*. Yes."

Casey waited expectantly.

Mrs. Thorrien said something very rapidly in French.

"What does that mean?"

"I like these pretty flowers."

Casey rolled her eyes at Walter and finished the rest of her pancakes.

8

It was a good thing Walter had an appointment with the dentist. From her bedroom window Casey had seen him drive away with his mother. She had thrown on some clothes and raced through breakfast, thinking this was the perfect time to try out his chinning bar. No sense letting him know she was determined to do more pull-ups than Jim Williams, the best athlete in the school—at least not until she had practiced a little.

She trotted down Walter's driveway and pulled open the heavy garage doors. Walter's mother and father certainly were the tidiest people in the neighborhood. Their tools and paint cans were stacked neatly on the shelves, and the rake and broom hung on hooks. Near the front of the garage, nailed to two beams, was the chinning bar.

She stood in front of it, eyes narrowed. Someday

Van would be standing on her head thinking she was some kind of athletic genius. And someone would come along and say, "Hey, have you heard about Casey? Forty-four pull-ups today and not even out of breath. I guess it must be hard to have a sister who's so terrific."

Slowly she spit on her hands and wiped them on her jeans. Stretching her arms over her head, she leaped for the bar. For a minute she hung there, swinging gently, before she tried to raise her head over the top.

Not too easy, she thought. She could only get the top of her head as high as the bar. No, not easy at all. She loosened her grip on the bar and collapsed on the garage floor.

"Never get to be a celebrity athlete this way," she said as she pushed herself to her feet.

"You can say that again," a voice said behind her.

She jumped and spun around. "Gunther Reed. Why are you spying on me?"

"Spying?" He grinned. "Ball went over the school-yard fence." He held it up. "Landed in the Moleses' backyard." He started down the driveway, then called back over his shoulder, "You, a celebrity?" Cackling horribly, he loped down the street toward his house.

"You big pineapple!" she yelled after him.

She turned and looked at the bar. "Lousy idea any-way. Have to think of something else. Too bad I can't knock out Gunther Reed's front teeth. Then I'd really be a celebrity. Probably even his mother wouldn't mind."

She stood for a minute trying to decide what she could do while she waited for Walter. Maybe she should dig up the fish, just check them out and see

She hung there, swinging gently.

what was doing with them. She took a step toward the Secret Passageway and hesitated. It really wouldn't be fair. She'd kill Walter if he dug them up without her.

Behind her she heard a car door slam. Quickly she dusted off her hands. "Back already?" she asked Walter as he trudged down the driveway toward her.

"Already?" He scowled. "You wouldn't have thought it was so fast if you'd been tortured by the dentist for an hour." He put his finger in his mouth and rubbed his gum gently.

She touched her own braces sympathetically. "You think I don't know? Best thing is not to think about it. Come on, let's look at the fish."

"Again? We dug them up the other day."

"So what? There's nothing else to do. Boringest Saturday morning I've had in ten years."

He hesitated. "I really should get my papers delivered early today. I want to stop and ask a lot of weekday people to take the Sunday paper."

"Why do you have to waste your time on that now? I've been hanging around this yard all morning. Not a thing to do, just waiting for you to get home."

"The kid who adds the most new customers to the Sunday paper gets a prize."

"Money?"

"No. You get to have lunch with the famous reporter Lance Levan."

"Really?"

"Yeah," Walter said. "The kid who won last year said it was the best lunch he ever had. He ate four desserts and started on a fifth. When he couldn't finish it, they packed it up in a box for him to take home."

"I guess everybody in the country knows Lance Levan's name," Casey said dreamily. "It must be something to be a famous reporter. Hey, I wonder—"

"What?"

"Let me think about it awhile. I have to ask Mrs. Petty if it's all right. It might be just what I'm looking for in this celebrity business. But listen, Walt, I've got to do something with myself this morning, and if you're so determined to sell newspapers, I'm going to dig up those fish by myself."

He stood there, undecided. Then he nodded. "Who am I kidding, anyway? After I go through a big speech with the first three customers, I'd be sick of the whole thing and give it up anyway. Wait till I get the shovel." He took down the spade that was hanging neatly against the garage wall. "Let's go."

They hurdled the fence and started to dig. Five minutes later they still hadn't found the bright red coffee can. "Strange," Walter said.

"Keep digging," Casey said. "Bound to be here. Same thing happened last time. There, I see the edge of it now."

"Yeah. But look where it is. We didn't put it all the way over here next to the fence."

"Don't be silly. We must have." She knelt down and pried out the can. "Sit down a minute and rest while I take a look."

He wiped his forehead and squatted next to the fence as she ran her fingers under the lid of the can.

"I hate to tell you," she said as she looked in the can, "but they don't seem to be in here."

He leaned over to look. "You're right. Holy moly. What's that?"

"A piece of slimy paper." She reached in under the lid, pulled it out, and read:

IF YOU WANT THEM BACK,

LEAVE 50¢ IN THE CAN.

SIGNED,

THE FISHNAPPER

HA. HA.

"Hey," she said, outraged. "What nerve!"

"Who—"

"Who do you think? I'll bet anything it was Goony Reed."

"Do you think so?"

"Of course. He's going to turn out to be a real criminal someday, if you ask me. We'll pick up the newspaper and there he'll be, smack on the front page." She tossed the can back into the hole. "Throw some dirt on it, Walt. Let him dig it up again before he finds out we didn't put the money in it."

Walter tossed a shovelful of dirt on the can. Leaning on the handle of the spade, he said, "He's really not so bad. Just wants to make you pay attention to him."

"He certainly doesn't know how to go about it."

Walter threw another pile of dirt over the hole and stamped on it.

Casey got up to help him flatten the dirt. "The whole world will know Gunther's name someday," she said. "I can see the headlines—'Gunther Reed Sentenced to

Life Imprisonment for Ripping off the First National Bank.' Yes, and I probably won't ever be a celebrity even in my own school."

"That reminds me." Walter reached into his pocket and brought out a crumpled piece of paper. "I've got something for you."

"I hope it's not another pen pal. I'm having enough trouble keeping up with Tracy Matson."

Walter shook his head. "No pen pal. It's from my grandmother. I forgot to give it to you."

She unfolded the paper and smoothed it out.

Dear Casey,
Here are some words for you. When you know them, I will be happy to give you some more.

Sincerely,
Marie Thorrien

The French word is:	You say it this way:	It means:
un . . . deux . . . trois	uhn . . . duh . . . trwah	1 . . . 2 . . . 3
Bonjour	bohn zhoor	hello
Au revoir	oh ra-vwahr	good-bye
Je m'appelle Casey.	Zhuh ma-pehl Casey.	My name is Casey.

Casey sat there, running her tongue along her braces. Then, flicking the paper with her index finger, she looked up at Walter. "Do you know anybody in the class who speaks French?"

He shook his head and threw a pebble through a hole in the fence.

"Darlene Pain-in-the-A Verona?"

"No."

"And how about my sister Van?"

"You know she doesn't—" he began and picked up another pebble.

"No," she said, answering her own question. "Nobody does except"—she paused and put her hands on her hips—"Zee Great Ca-sey, Fourth Grade Cee-le-bri-ty."

He tossed another pebble at a tree on the other side of the fence and grunted.

She stood up and dusted off her pants. "See you later. I'm going in the house to memorize these words. Get hold of your grandmother as soon as you can. Tell her to write out a new list. Tell her she can put twice as many words on the next list. Get it for tomorrow. And, Walt—"

"Yeah?"

"Tell her to write some sentences. Some nice long important sentences."

She stuck one foot into a hole in the Cyclone fence and swung the other leg over the top. "Oh ra-vwahr, old boy, I'll see you later."

9

As the class filed out of the room at lunchtime on Monday, Casey paused at the classroom door. She took one last look at the list Walter had given her this morning from his grandmother. She had almost memorized the twelve new French words on it. Mrs. Petty was still sitting at her desk marking the English compositions they had done that morning. Casey wondered if she ever ate lunch. She certainly was fat enough to skip it.

"What is it, Cassandra?" Mrs. Petty asked, looking up.

Casey cleared her throat. "I was thinking about getting a newspaper together—sell it to the kids in school —get some money for the class treasury for trips and stuff."

"That's a very good idea," Mrs. Petty said in a slightly surprised voice.

"But we'd need some help," Casey went on. "Paper and permission to use the ditto machine in the office."

Mrs. Petty reached into her desk drawer and pulled out a bulging paper bag. "That shouldn't be much of a problem." She put a fat ham hero and two packages of chocolate crackers on the desk. Casey's mouth watered.

"I guess you'd like me to be the editor," Mrs. Petty suggested.

"Er, not exactly. I thought, being the class president and all, that I'd—"

Mrs. Petty took a bite of the sandwich and started to chew. "This English composition you wrote this morning doesn't seem to be the work of a newspaper editor."

"I couldn't think of anything I did over the weekend that was interesting enough to write about."

Mrs. Petty sat there rolling the hunk of sandwich from one side of her mouth to the other. She swallowed. "All right," she said at last. "Get a committee together and let's see how it goes."

"I will," Casey answered, relieved. "Right away."

"Make sure you get some people who can write well. Like Darlene, perhaps."

Casey nodded.

"And ask Gunther."

"Gunther Reed?"

"Be sure to put him in on this. Be good for him."

She leaned over and took another bite of sandwich. "This newspaper business may teach you a little effi-

Casey's mouth watered.

ciency also, Cassandra. Now go down and get some lunch before the hour is up."

Casey sped down to the cafeteria, her sneakers pounding on the stairs. That Gunther Reed. That turkey.

She grabbed up a tray and slipped into the lunch line, making a face at the gooey chow mein Betty dumped on her plate.

When she got to the fourth-grade table, she pushed hard against Mindy to make room and slid onto the edge of the bench. "Listen, kids," she said. "We're going to have a class newspaper."

No one heard her. All the kids were hunched over their plates, trying to slide the chow mein onto their forks.

"Hey, listen." She took her fork and banged on the side of her tray.

Darlene looked up and nudged the girls on each side of her with her elbows.

"We're going to have a class newspaper," Casey repeated when most of the kids stopped talking. "Mrs. Petty said we could. Everybody can write for it, but we need a committee who'll do most of the work." She paused to take a sip of milk. "I'm supposed to pick the committee."

Suddenly everyone was quiet. She looked down the table questioningly at Walter, but he shook his head. No surprise. Walter hated anything to do with writing.

Darlene leaned across the table. "Pick me," she whispered. "Come on."

Casey narrowed her eyes and looked at her.

"That reminds me," Darlene continued. "I forgot to

47

ask you to my birthday party. Completely slipped my mind."

Casey hesitated. Then when Darlene had almost given up, she said, "*Naturellement*, my dear Darlene, I was going to ask you anyway. And . . . I'll come to your party, too." She tried not to giggle.

She looked around the table again. It was clear that Mindy was dying to be picked. Good idea actually. Mindy would be the only one who wouldn't fight to be boss. "Mindy," she said, and was pleased to see Mindy's face light up. "One more, I guess," she said, delaying, hating to add Gunther to the group.

At last she looked at him. "How about you, Goony?"

He pretended to fall backward off the bench.

"Well," she said grudgingly, "Mrs. Petty suggested—"

For a moment he didn't answer. Then: "I might have known. Mrs. Petty said I had to be on the committee. Right?"

She ignored him. "We have to get together to have a meeting. How about my house on Friday?"

"Why wait so long?" Darlene asked.

"House is being painted. I'm not allowed to have kids in while my father is painting. Ladders and stuff all over the place."

"We don't have to have it at your house," Gunther said.

"He's right," Darlene agreed. "Let's not wait so long."

"Uh-uh," Casey said. If they went to his house, he'd be able to hog the whole thing. "I'm the editor. We'll have it at my house. Keep the records and stuff there."

48

Gunther laughed rudely. "Watch out or you'll be the editor of a newspaper that nobody will pay any attention to. I'll start a rival one."

Mindy looked nervous. "Let's not ruin this before it even gets a chance to get started."

"My house this afternoon?" asked Gunther.

"Good idea," Darlene said.

Casey glanced around the table and sighed. "All right," she said. "You win, Goony. This time."

10

Casey quick-stepped down 199th Street, trying to catch up with Gunther and Darlene. "Hurry, Mindy," she said over her shoulder. "If Goony gets it into his head that he can run this whole thing, my newspaper idea will be ruined."

Gunther took a shortcut across his front lawn. "Come on, gang," he yelled, climbing the steps. He leaned on the bell until his mother came to the door.

Casey was surprised to see Mrs. Reed up close. She looked like a perfectly ordinary woman. Certainly not the kind of person to have a kid like Gunther. She wondered if Mrs. Reed realized how revolting her son was, jumping around the hall with his filthy shirt hanging out all over the place.

But Mrs. Reed didn't seem to notice. She ran her hand over Gunther's head as she smiled and invited them into the living room. It was a sunny room, all yellow and green, Casey noticed. She wished her mother had as much style as Mrs. Reed.

"A newspaper?" Mrs. Reed said after Gunther told her why they were there. "What a perfectly wonderful idea."

"It was mine," Casey said. She wanted to make sure they kept everything straight right from the beginning.

Goony leered at her. "This is Casey, Mom. She's the one I told you about, the one who wants to be a celebrity."

Casey's face burned. She could hardly look at Mrs. Reed. "Well, if we're here," she mumbled, "we might as well get to work."

Mrs. Reed laughed. "Don't let him bother you, Casey. He really admires you a lot." She turned to the door and said over her shoulder, "I'll be right back with some soda."

Casey looked at Gunther curiously. He slowly crossed his eyes and stuck his finger up his nose.

She shuddered. "You're really disgusting." Then she turned her back on him and spoke to the others. "I thought if we looked at a real newspaper first, we could write down a list of things we could include in our own."

Darlene nodded. "Do you have any old newspapers, Goony?" She unzipped her schoolbag and took out a pencil and paper. "I'll make the list."

"No, that's all right," Casey answered quickly. "I have a pencil right here." She fumbled in her pocketbook. "Get the newspaper, Goony."

"Did you ever notice," he said, "that everyone wants

to be the boss around here? And nobody wants to be just a plain worker?"

"Oh, shut up and get the paper," Casey said.

He stood up and sauntered out to the hall. "Here you are, Tinsel Teeth," he yelled. The paper came sailing across the room.

Casey reached for it and handed it to Mindy. Better give her something to do, she thought. If Mindy got bored and went home, they'd lose the only plain worker they had in the whole place.

Mindy knelt on the floor and spread the paper around her. "Well," she began, "there's the news of what's going on in the world—"

"Wait a minute," Casey broke in. "How about the title first? We'd better decide on a name for ourselves."

"How about 'Fourth-Grade News'?" Mindy suggested.

"Terrible," Casey and Darlene answered at once.

Goony looked at Casey. "How about 'Gunther's Goodies'?"

Mindy giggled. Casey didn't bother to answer.

"It really has to have something like 'Telegram' or 'Herald' or 'Observer' in it," Darlene said.

"Good idea." Casey nodded approvingly. "How about 'The Ogden School Observer'?"

Darlene looked up at the ceiling, considering. Finally she began to write in her notebook. "Yes," she said. "That looks good."

"I told you I'd do the writing," Casey said.

"No harm in both doing it," Darlene answered. "Actually it's better that way. Otherwise you might lose our only copy."

Casey smoothed out her paper and wrote in large letters:

THE OGDEN SCHOOL OBSERVER

EDITED BY CASSANDRA ELEANOR VALENTINE

She held the paper in the air for Darlene to see. "Do you know how to spell my name?"

"Look here, Casey," Darlene said. "There's no need for your name to be hanging up there right on top. We're all doing the work. If you think I'm going to spend all my time writing this newspaper and not get any of the credit, you're crazy."

"I think she's right, Casey," Mindy said. "Why don't we make a box on the bottom of the first page with all our names in it. Yours can be first and say 'editor' after it."

"It was my idea—"

Gunther broke in. "I guess you've said that only about twenty-five times in the last ten minutes."

"All right." She glared at him as she crossed her name out under the title.

Mindy turned a page of the newspaper. "Don't forget about sports and recipes."

Casey wrote furiously.

"Don't forget obituaries." Gunther snickered, looking over Mindy's shoulder as she turned a page.

"What's that?" Mindy asked.

"When you die, you get to have your name in the paper," he answered.

"Keep acting like a turkey and you'll be the first one in that section," Casey said.

53

"I've been shot by Boss Tinsel Teeth," Gunther yelled and dropped to the floor. "Shot right in the—"

"Gunther," his mother said from the doorway, "cut that out and take this tray."

He got to his feet, took the tray of sodas from his mother, and set it down.

"Behave yourself," she said and disappeared down the hall.

"Yeah," Casey said. "Come on, be serious, *mes amis.* I'd really like to get this thing started."

Mindy nodded seriously. "It's nearly four thirty. It'll be time to go home soon."

"We can't just go home," Casey said, annoyed. "Don't you know anything about a real newspaper? Haven't you heard about deadlines?"

Gunther held up his arms. "All right. I surrender." He sank back to the floor. "What do you want me to do?"

"I guess you could be a reporter. Wander around the school and the neighborhood looking for news."

"Right," Darlene said. "Anything important that happens or anything interesting."

"Even if it happens at the last minute," Mindy said. "You know we could stop the press and add it right in."

"You mean stop the ditto machine," Casey said.

"Okay, I get it," Gunther said. "What are the rest of you going to do?"

"I'll write a society column," Darlene put in quickly. "I guess I'd be the best qualified to do that."

"All right," Casey said. She'd better not make a fuss in case Darlene changed her mind about inviting her to the birthday party. "Since I'm the editor I'll run the whole thing. Ask Walter to write something about the weather maybe. We might do something about science. Then all we have to do is put it together, write it up, learn how to use the ditto machine, and—"

"Yes," Darlene interrupted loudly. "I'll be the society reporter. Good thing my party is coming up. That's the first thing that'll go into the column."

11

"Hey, wait up," Casey yelled to Walter the next afternoon. He was halfway across the schoolyard on his way home. She shifted her books under her arm and raced to catch up with him.

"*Bonjour*," she said a little breathlessly. "Important afternoon coming up."

"Bone sur," he answered. "Why?"

"It's finally Darlene's party day. Thought it would never come. Can't wait to get home to see what my mother bought for her. I told her to get something special, something with—you know—class."

"A celebrity present?"

"You got it. Exactly."

"Why didn't you go with her?"

"Forgot about the present until this morning. Besides"—she kicked a stone out of the way—"I couldn't think of anything myself."

She waved good-bye as Walter turned up his path; then she cut across her front lawn. Throwing open the back door, she called, "Hey, anybody home here?"

Her mother appeared at the kitchen door, finger on her lips. "Ssh, Van's sleeping. She was sent home sick from school an hour ago."

"What's the matter?"

"Sore throat, I think."

"Probably just sick of school, if you ask me." Casey tossed her books on the kitchen chair. "Did you get a present for Darlene?"

Her mother nodded. "On the dining-room table. I didn't wrap it yet. Thought you might like to see it first."

Casey took a doughnut off the plate on top of the refrigerator. "What did you get?" she asked.

"A game. It was on sale at Breen's."

Casey wandered into the dining room. There was a cardboard box on the table. Written in large red letters across the yellow-and-orange box were the words: STANDOUT: A GAME FOR ALL AGES. She picked it up and listened to the pieces rattling inside. "More like a game for two-year-olds," she muttered. "I'd be laughed right out of the party if I brought something like this."

"Did you say something, Casey?" her mother called.

She cleared her throat. "I think Darlene may have this game already."

"Oh, dear." Her mother came into the dining room. "It's really too late to get anything else now. I'm sure Breen's will exchange it for her."

"I guess so," Casey said slowly. She laid the box gently on the table. "I'm going up to change."

"Try not to wake Van."

Casey went slowly up the stairs. She had about ten minutes to find a way out of this mess. Her mother was right. There was no time to buy another present. She'd have to find something of her own. But what?

She tiptoed into the bedroom and looked around. On her dresser were two stuffed animals that she had won at a carnival in August, but they seemed a little gray and dusty. Besides, she wasn't sure Darlene would be interested in a pair of lavender pandas. She opened her dresser drawer and poked around, looking at her jewelry. She held a silver bracelet up to the light but quickly dropped it back into its cotton nest. The clasp was broken and one of the stones had fallen out.

Then she spotted the necklace. It was perfect. Made of square wooden beads, it was the color of beach sand on a sunny day.

There was only one problem. The necklace was Van's. In fact, when she ran the beads through her fingers, she noticed that a brown V was stamped on the center bead. V for Van. Could just as well be V for Verona.

She turned toward the lump in the middle of Van's bed. "Vanny?"

"Mmm?"

"Can I have your brown bead necklace?"

The lump moved a little. "No."

"You never use it. It's a stupid-looking thing—old as the hills."

She ran the beads through her fingers.

"Mmm." The lump settled itself and was still.

Casey stood there, considering, not sure whether Van's "Mmm" meant yes or no. It meant yes, she decided at last. She tossed the necklace in the air with one hand and grabbed for it with the other.

She missed. The necklace clattered on the edge of the radiator and dropped behind it to the floor.

"Will you get out of here, Casey?" Van grumbled. "What a pest you are."

"Shut up, brat face," she answered good-humoredly. She grabbed the necklace and skipped back downstairs to get the wrapping paper.

She was ready in twenty minutes. Dressed in new gray slacks with Van's yellow scarf tied in a knot around her collar, she tucked two neatly wrapped packages under her arm and started down the street. Walter was sitting on his front steps, head bent over a pen and notebook.

She walked up his path. "Doing homework?"

"I'm working on the experiment book. Trying to think of something else now that the fish are gone. Maybe we could get some water, raise some mosquitoes or larvae or something."

"Too late, I think—nearly winter," she said. "Plenty of other things to do, though, now that my newspaper idea worked out. Weather observations, stuff like that." She paused. "Listen, Walt, do me a favor? Hide this in your garage." She handed him the Standout game.

"Why?"

"Don't want to hurt my mother's feelings." She sighed. "It's too late to explain now. I'm late for Darlene's party. Stinky, ratty wrapping paper in our house. Ribbon's been used fifty times. Had to look all over the place to find one decent piece."

Walter nodded and started for the garage.

"I'll see you later," she called over her shoulder and rushed down 200th Street. At the corner she turned left and jaywalked across the street, dodging a car whose driver sounded a long, angry blast on his horn.

"Yah-hoo to you, mister." She crossed her eyes and waggled her tongue after him.

When she reached 202nd Street, she stopped to catch her breath, then strode up Darlene's front path and leaned on the bell. Lucky Darlene. It was the chime kind. Loud too. She rang it again quickly so she could listen. Eight rings: a ding, ding, dong, two deep bongs, then up again with a dong and two dings. A celebrity-type bell.

After a minute she stood on tiptoe to look in the little window next to the door to see why no one was coming. She jumped back as she heard a rush of feet down the hall.

The door burst open. Darlene stood there with half the fourth-grade girls in back of her. She held out her hand for Casey's present, then turned and ran back to her living room. Shouting and laughing, the girls followed.

Casey raced into the house in back of them. "*Bonjour, mes amis*," she shouted. "Your president and editor is here."

"Big deal. And what's this *bonjour* business?" Darlene asked.

61

"It happens that I'm learning French."

Linda Abel looked up from the floor, where she was leaning against the blue-and-green-striped couch. "Hey, Casey, you're lucky.

"I'll teach you if you—"

"How about we discuss that some other time?" Darlene cut in. "Right now I want to get to my presents." She reached for a package and tore the paper off in large strips.

"Gorgeous," she said, holding up a tan leather change purse. She dropped it back into its box and passed it around for the girls to admire.

Casey dug into the nut dish on the table next to her, and tossed a pile of nuts into her mouth.

Darlene peered into the next box. "Nice," she said indifferently, looking at Mindy's present. Casey leaned over to take a look. She recognized the yellow-and-orange box even before she saw the word *Standout* written across the front. One of the playing pieces fell out of the box and rolled under a chair. She noticed that Darlene didn't even bother to reach for the little green disk. She knew it. It was a crummy present.

She watched Mindy scramble under the chair, grab the piece, and drop it back into the box. Poor Mindy didn't have one ounce of style.

In no time Darlene was surrounded by a mound of wrapping paper and ribbons and opened boxes. Finally she picked up the long, narrow box that Casey had brought. She glanced at the card taped to the top of the package and tore into the blue-and-green wrapping paper. Casey pretended to be interested in a pink piggy bank that Joanne Palmer had brought.

"Gorgeous," Darlene shouted. Casey swiveled her head around to see Darlene holding up the chunky brown necklace. "Where did you get the beads," she asked, "and how did you ever string them?" She pulled the beads apart to show everyone the intricate knots between each bead while Casey sat there, stunned. Handmade!

Joanne grabbed the necklace. "How clever of you, Casey! I knew Gunther Reed was wrong about you."

"Gunther?"

"He said that Van was the only Valentine with style."

"He said that?" Casey asked, outraged.

"Don't be mad," Joanne said. She reached for the box and dropped the necklace into it. "Anybody who could make a necklace like that doesn't have to worry about having style."

Before Casey could answer, Darlene's older sister, Sue, appeared in the doorway. "Mom says the cake and ice cream are ready."

Darlene stood up and turned to Casey. "You'll have to come over tomorrow. Teach us all how to make jewelry. Maybe we could write up the directions in our newspaper. Have a handcraft column."

Casey gulped and nodded. Darlene led the way into the dining room.

12

Dear Tracy,

When I got home from Darlene's party this afternoon, I found another letter from you. You sure write a lot.

Everybody wanted to sit next to me at the party. They are so thrilled when I teach them how to say some words in French.

I bought Darlene a necklace. Her mother wanted to lock it up in a safe because she said it probably cost more than the whole house, but I said don't be silly, *ma chère*, it's nothing.

As usual, I'm very busy. We are going to have a class newspaper (my idea). Guess who is going to be the editor?

Love,
Cassandra Eleanor

13

Casey hung her raincoat on the hook and snapped the clothespin over her boots to keep them together. Usually she loved a rainy day in school. The classroom always seemed so bright and cozy when everything was dark and gloomy outside.

But what had started out to be a great day was certainly turning into a horrible mess. One of her boots had a hole in the toe so her sock was wet and clammy, and her rain hat had blown off, plastering her bangs to her forehead.

But that was the least of her troubles.

The problem was Van, or at least what Van had told her. Every time she thought about it, she couldn't make up her mind whether to giggle hysterically or just die of embarrassment.

She'd awakened early this morning before the alarm

had rung and watched the rain pelt the window. Then she stretched and looked over toward her sister's bed.

Finally Van opened her eyes.

Casey leaned up on her elbow. "How do you feel?"

"Not well enough to go to school."

"You're about as sick as . . ." She paused, then began again. "I mean that's too bad. Hey, Vanny, you know that bead necklace you gave me?"

"I thought I told you not to touch that."

"I took it. You don't mind, do you?"

"I certainly do," Van said.

"I'll give you a dollar when I get some money. But right now I need to know how to make it."

Van shrugged. "Who knows?"

"I'm not kidding." Casey slipped out of bed and began to dress. "Darlene invited me over this afternoon. I want to show her how you made it."

"Are you crazy? I didn't make that necklace."

Casey popped the last button through the hole and stared, mouth open. "What are you talking about?"

Van punched her pillow and settled back. "Listen, Casey, I'm trying to sleep. I just said I didn't string that necklace. But as long as you're going to Darlene Verona's this afternoon, ask her sister Susan."

"Why should I do that?"

"She made it for me last Christmas."

Casey stared at her sister in horror. "You big creep," she said. "You let me give that to Darlene for a birthday present?"

"You what?" Van began to laugh. "Serves you right."

Now, squaring her shoulders, Casey marched out of the classroom closet and slid into her seat just as Mrs.

Petty tapped on her desk for order. Casey tore a piece of paper out of her assignment pad, licked the point of her pencil, and began to write.

Walter:
Urgent. Meet me in the hall *tout de suite*.
(Right away!)

C.

Nonchalantly she strolled to the corner of the room to sharpen her pencil. She dropped the note on Walter's desk as she passed. Five minutes later he signed his initials on the blackboard for the boys' room, and two minutes after that she signed hers under the girls' column. She rushed down the hall to the water fountain, where Walter was waiting.

"I'm dead, Walt," she said. "Finished."

"What's up?"

Quickly she told him about the necklace.

"You'd have been better off giving her the Standout game instead of leaving it in my garage to get greasy."

"Don't waste time about that now. What am I going to do?"

"You're dead. As you say, finished. That's the end of your celebrity life."

"Look, Walt, I don't need the jokes right now."

He leaned over the water fountain and slurped down a long drink. Then he looked up. "You'll think of something. Make up a story. You're getting pretty good at that." He wiped his mouth with the back of his hand, grinned at her, then loped back to the classroom.

For a few moments she stood looking after him.

Then she leaned down for a quick drink. She walked back slowly.

As soon as she could, she got up from her seat and went to the pencil sharpener again. This time she dropped a note on Darlene's desk.

Dear D:

What good luck you're wearing my necklace, *ma petite*. Lend it back to me so I can show the man in the store which beads I want. (They have to be ordered. They come from Bangkok.)

C.

P.S. I'll still come over today.
P.S. Again. Did your sister see the necklace?

She sharpened her pencil until it was a little stub, so that Darlene would have a chance to answer her note. On the way back she reached out and grabbed the necklace and the folded piece of paper that Darlene held out to her. Sliding back into her seat, she unfolded the paper.

C:

Tell the man to hurry up and order the beads. I didn't show my sister your necklace. I hate her guts.

D.

Mrs. Petty looked up from her desk. "You seem to have a lot of trouble getting down to business this morning, Cassandra."

Casey smiled slightly and nodded. "I'm just about ready to begin now. I hope."

14

Dear Tracy,

I received your letter when I got home from school today. I didn't get home until late because I was at Darlene's house. We were talking about our class newspaper all afternoon. It will probably turn out to be great—that is if a gross boy in my class named Gunther Reed doesn't ruin the whole thing.

It was nice of you to invite me to your house next summer. You're pretty lucky to be able to go swimming and fishing whenever you like. Do you like to eat fish? (I don't.)

Of course, I wouldn't mind sleeping in a regular-type house. In fact, it would be a nice change after sleeping in a mansion all my life. Too bad you live so far away or I'd take you up on it. Maybe when I get older.

"Dear Tracy, I received your letter."

And maybe you can visit me here. I have six bathrooms and seven fireplaces and an in-ground swimming pool, so there's plenty of room. Maybe you can come when you're about twenty or thirty. By that time you may be able to speak French so you can talk to our downstairs maid.

Write soon, *ma chère*.

Love,
Cassandra Eleanor

15

After dismissal on Friday Mrs. Petty led the newspaper staff into the ditto room. Casey dumped her coat on top of a table and leaned against the wall with the rest of the committee. She took a long, deep breath. There was nothing in the world that smelled as good as ditto ink, unless you counted the smell of gasoline at Albano's Service Station.

She yawned, sat on the table, and swung her legs back and forth, trying to stay awake, as she listened to Mrs. Petty explain how to use the ditto machine. Teachers always seemed to repeat things over and over.

"It's very simple," Mrs. Petty said. "After you have written the article on a special type of paper called a ditto master, you are ready to begin. Turn on the machine, put your ditto master in it, set the button for the number of copies you want, then stand back. In a few minutes the copies will fall into a tray under the machine. Cassandra?"

Casey looked up.

"Suppose you tell us what to do after you have written your article on a ditto master."

Glad to be doing something besides just listening, Casey stood up and repeated swiftly, "Put the ditto master in the machine, set the button for the copies, and they'll come out on the bottom."

"You've got it." Mrs. Petty nodded approvingly.

"Not quite," Gunther said, smirking at Casey. "One little detail. She forgot to turn on the machine."

Mrs. Petty sighed. "That will do, Gunther." Then briskly she said, "Now let's get to the newspaper itself." She looked around the table. "Do all of you have your articles ready?"

Darlene pulled out a pile of papers. "I have my stuff right here." She turned to Casey. "That reminds me— did you write up the directions for the beads to put in the paper?"

Casey flushed. "Not yet."

"What beads?" Gunther asked.

"Casey gave me a necklace for my birthday. She made it herself with imported beads—from Bangkok."

Gunther rolled his eyes and grinned at Casey.

It was pretty hard to fool Gunther, she thought. "I think I'll save the directions for another issue," she said, glaring at him.

"How's your article coming, Mindy?" Mrs. Petty asked.

"I'm almost finished. I should be able to have it ready by tomorrow."

Mrs. Petty looked at the rest of them. They nodded.

"Well, everything seems to be coming along very nicely. You should be able to earn a good bit for the class treasury. Have you thought about how much you want to charge for each copy?"

"Not too much," Casey answered. "Otherwise no one will buy it. Maybe ten cents?"

"That sounds right," Darlene agreed. "I hope we sell a lot."

"Maybe we ought to do something to make everyone interested in buying the paper. Advertise it or something."

"We could put posters around," Mindy suggested.

"Nah," Gunther said. "Posters all over the school now. Nobody even bothers to read them."

"Even so," Mrs. Petty said, "I think you might make a few."

"I'll do that." Mindy looked around. The rest of them were glad Mindy wanted to do the work.

"How about a prize?" Casey asked. "We could sell chances and—" She paused to think. "Yes. We could sell chances for a nickel, and the winner could be announced in the first issue of the paper." She looked around. "How does that sound?"

"Not bad," Gunther said.

"Terrific," Mindy agreed.

"Yes," Mrs. Petty said. "I think you've really got an excellent idea."

"What can we use for a prize?" Darlene asked.

"We'll think of something," Casey said.

"I'm sure you will," Mrs. Petty said. "In the mean-time you can practice using the ditto machine by running off an advertisement and some chances right now." She handed Casey a ruler, a pencil, and a ditto master.

Casey thought for a moment, then wrote carefully:

TAKE A CHANCE ON

A MYSTERY PRIZE

ONLY FIVE CENTS

WINNER WILL BE ANNOUNCED

IN

The Ogden School Observer

FIRST ISSUE ON SALE NEXT MONDAY

Casey held it up for everyone to see. "We can run lots of these off and put them around the school."

She took a second ditto master and divided it into boxes. In large letters she wrote: MYSTERY CHANCE. Underneath she drew a line. "We can put the person's name in here," she said, pointing to the line.

"Very nice," Mrs. Petty said. "Let's see if you can run them off now."

Slowly Casey attached the first ditto master to the machine and turned it on. In no time, copies of the advertisement lay in neat piles in front of them. Casey removed the first ditto master, attached the second, and ran off the chances.

"Well," said Mrs. Petty, "that settles that. Now don't forget to give me your articles within the next day or two so I can correct them."

Gunther raised his hand. "I've got a great idea. It

just so happens that I have a typewriter. I could type up everybody's stories."

Mrs. Petty nodded slowly. "I must say, Gunther, that it would be a nice touch to have everything typed up neatly."

Gunther went on. "I'm the roving reporter, too, you know, the one who goes around looking for current events. I have a lot to do on this paper."

Casey looked at Mindy. "Big deal," she mouthed.

Mrs. Petty clapped her hands to get their attention. "I think that does it now. Get your articles to Gunther and he can type them up over the weekend. I'll give you time off Monday to leave class and use the ditto room. Right now"—she looked at her watch—"I have to go back to the classroom for my things. You may put on your coats and dismiss yourselves. Quietly." She turned and clumped out of the room.

Gunther leaned over to Casey. "I can see the roving reporter's headlines now: 'Class President Digs Up Dead Fish for Dinner.' "

"You wouldn't dare, Goony."

"That's a chance you'll have to take." He snickered. "Read all about it in *The Ogden School Observer*."

"That really wouldn't be fair, Gunther," Darlene said, but Casey could see she was trying hard not to laugh.

Casey edged off the table and picked up her coat. "Gunther," she began, "you—"

He stared off into space. " 'Casey Valentine in Love with Gunther Reed,' " he said. Then he grabbed up his coat and ran down the hall, with Casey five steps behind him.

Gunther raced down the steps.

"If I catch you, I'll kill you!" she yelled.

Gunther raced down the steps in front of the school. He nearly collided with two women who stood on the path waiting for their children. "Sorry," he called over his shoulder. "That girl is crazy about me. Keeps chasing me. Won't let me alone."

The women looked up the stairs toward Casey. She stopped running and, gritting her teeth, ducked behind the stone pillar on the top of the steps and waited. When she peeked out, Gunther had turned the corner, and the women had collected their children and were halfway down the block.

Casey went back into the school. She had something to do.

16

That night Casey dashed down the stairs ahead of Van and caught the phone on the second ring. "For me, *naturellement*," she said. She pulled the phone into the hall closet and shut the door behind her. "Is that you, Walt? Sorry your mother had to get you out of bed."

"Yeah. You'd better make it fast. She's having a fit. She wants to know what you're doing up so late anyway."

"I've been on the phone since supper, talking to people about the newspaper."

"Hey, I'm half asleep . . ."

"Stay awake a minute, will you, Walt? This is important. At the meeting this afternoon we decided to sell chances for a prize."

"That's why you had to call at eleven o'clock? You

could have told me that tomorrow. We have the whole weekend."

"Listen, Walter, if I know Darlene and Gunther, they'll try to sell chances to all the kids before I'm even out of bed in the morning." She ran her tongue over her braces. "Well, they're going to get some surprise."

"Do you really think anyone is going to buy a chance?"

"Sure. Why not? Walt, this paper just has to be a success. My whole campaign to get myself known around the school depends on it."

"A chance on what, anyway? And how much?"

"Five cents. And Darlene wanted to make the prize a necklace made of genuine beads from Bangkok."

"Wow."

"Wow is right. That reminds me, I wanted to tell you I buried that necklace in the fish can just before supper. I never want to see that thing again." She leaned back against a coat hanging on a hook. "It took about four phone calls to straighten that out. Darlene had already called Gunther and Mindy with that suggestion. Anyway, I finally persuaded them to make the first prize—Walter, are you still there? Walt? Wake up."

"Couldn't we just run through this whole thing tomorrow, Casey?"

"Yeah, sure. Just get up early. We've got a lot of things to take care of in the morning. Got to get into the school somehow."

"On Saturday? What are you—crazy?"

"Never mind that now. Just meet me out in front at

eight o'clock." Gently she put the phone back on the hook, opened the closet door, and went upstairs.

Van was practicing sit-ups in front of the window. "What are you up to now, Casey?" she asked.

"Nothing much. Walter and I are going to sell chances tomorrow."

Van yawned. "Might know it would be something crazy if you and Walter are involved in it."

"Shut up, will you?"

"Hey, Casey, what's that out in the backyard? Looks like a flashlight."

Casey leaned over her shoulder. "You're right. It is a light. Maybe it's a robber. We'd better call Daddy."

"Wait a minute. That's not in the yard. It's in the Secret Passageway. Looks like some kid with a shovel."

Casey drew in her breath sharply. "It's that peabrain, Gunther Reed. And he's trying to dig up—" She stuck her head out the window as far as she could.

"Hey," she half whispered, half shouted, "Goony Reed. I see you out there."

"What's the matter with him?" Van asked, popping her head out next to Casey. "It must be nearly eleven o'clock. What's he doing?"

"Goony, I mean it," Casey whispered as loud as she could. "In a minute I'm going to scream and everyone in the neighborhood will be out there."

"How do you know it's Goony?" Van asked.

"I know," Casey answered firmly. "There he goes now."

They watched as the dark form, bent nearly double, climbed the fence and disappeared across the schoolyard. A neighbor's dog started to bark, and Mrs. Moles's bedroom light went on.

"Kid's got the whole town awake," Van observed. "What a nut."

"Did he get it—I mean did he have anything in his hand besides the shovel?"

"What?"

"Never mind. I'll be right back."

"Where are you going?"

"Bathroom." She tiptoed out of the bedroom and crept down the stairs. Groping around on the hall table, she found the light and switched it on. Swiftly she opened the telephone book and ran her finger down under the R's.

"Three-five-nine-two, three-five-nine-two," she mumbled to herself as she pulled the phone into the hall closet.

She dialed, then listened impatiently to the buzzing. On the thirteenth ring someone fumbled the phone off the hook.

"Mr. Reed?" Casey asked in a deep voice.

"Who is this?"

"This is a concerned citizen."

"Wha'?" he mumbled in a voice that seemed barely awake.

"I believe your son is prowling around the neighborhood."

"Wha'?" he asked again.

Casey could hear another voice in the background. "Who is that, Roscoe?"

"Prowling around the neighborhood," Casey repeated. "With a shovel. And a flashlight."

"Who is this, anyway?"

"Don't worry. He should be getting home any minute."

Gently she put down the telephone and stood in the hall, giggling. Served the fink right if they skinned him alive. She picked at her braces. She just hoped she had surprised him before he had gotten that necklace dug up. That would be all she'd need. Stupid thing to have buried it there in the first place, she thought as she climbed the stairs.

Van poked her head out from under the blanket as Casey got into bed. "Hey, you never told me what you're going to give for a prize."

"A game. It's called Standout. Actually, Mindy gave it to Darlene for her birthday, but Darlene was generous enough to donate it to a worthy cause."

17

The sun had just appeared over the houses on 200th Street when Casey crossed the driveway between her house and Walter's. She clutched a large envelope to her chest and huddled against the side of Walter's house.

While she waited, she pried the dirt out from under her fingernails. She had spent the last ten minutes digging in the Secret Passageway. The necklace was there! She had scared Gunther away in time.

She squinted up at Walter's window and shivered. It certainly was taking him long enough to get dressed and downstairs.

Finally he appeared.

"By the time we get started, it'll be suppertime," she complained.

He held out half an English muffin dripping with butter and leaned against the house next to her. "What's this all about, anyway?" he asked. "And what's in that envelope?"

She took the muffin and licked some butter off the top. "I'll tell you all about it after we get into the school."

"You'll get us expelled yet," he said.

"We're not going to commit a crime. I just want to take care of a few things that we can't do with a million teachers and kids around to slow things down." She wiped the crumbs off her mouth. "That was good. I didn't bother with breakfast this morning. Let's go."

"How do you think we're going to get in the building? Leo, the custodian, says he locks everything up tight as a drum every night."

"Leo's lucky a real burglar doesn't want to get into the school. He'd be out of his custodian's job fast if Mr. Rosenstrauss ever found out what Leo means by locking up."

She trotted ahead of Walter across the schoolyard. "I opened the grating in the cafeteria window after dismissal yesterday afternoon. Leo was so busy rushing around sweeping up so he could get out early that he never even looked to see what I was doing."

"Will you tell me what we're going to do in there? You want me to risk my neck and I don't even know what I'm doing it for."

Casey knelt in front of the grating and folded it back against the side of the brick wall, then slid the cafeteria window open. "Let's get inside first, then I'll tell you

85

all about it." She swung her legs over the sill and jumped down on a table. "Come on. We'll head for Mrs. Fiedler's room first."

Walter sat on a bench and shook his head. "No good."

"What do you mean?"

"I mean I'm not moving until you tell me what's going on."

She sighed. "Nothing but waste time this morning. All right." She brushed her bangs off her forehead. "We go up to the sixth grade—Mrs. Fiedler's. I heard Van say that she had a class list in her desk. All we have to do is borrow it and we've got the names and addresses of every kid in the sixth grade. Then all we have to do is go to their houses and sell them chances."

"Crazy," Walter muttered. "Why is it so important to sell chances to six-graders?"

"Can't you figure anything out, Walt? Darlene and Gunther will never think of selling to them. They'll concentrate on the fourth grade. Not only will we sell more chances this way, but I'll be able to introduce myself to everybody as Casey Valentine, the president of the fourth grade and editor of the brand-new paper *The Ogden School Observer*." She pushed open the cafeteria doors. "Everyone in the school will know me, and for the first time in my life that snooty old Van won't be ahead of me."

Reluctantly Walter followed her up the stairs. "Just a quick stop in the office, Walt," she said. "The teachers hang their keys on a rack every night. We'll pick up Mrs. Fiedler's and—"

"And?"

"Pick up the keys to the ditto room, too."

"Now what?"

"Walter, the whole day is slipping right through our fingers while you pot around making a fuss over every idea I have."

She went into the office and grabbed the keys before he had a chance to answer.

When she came out of the office, Walter waved at her wildly. She paused and looked over the edge of the staircase and out the large window on the stairs to where Walter was pointing.

"Here comes Leo with his keys." Walter whispered in a strangled voice. "He probably comes in every Saturday to make sure no one is in here."

"Hurry," she said.

They raced up the stairs to the third floor. They could hear Leo moving around downstairs, whistling while he opened a door.

They sped down the hall to the sixth-grade room. "Hold this," Casey said, handing Walter the envelope. She looked at Mrs. Fiedler's keys. There were six of them on the ring. "Nutty teachers. Always have a hundred keys when they need about two." Her hands shook as she tried one key after another. Walter jiggled up and down on his toes, watching the stairs over his shoulder. "He's coming up the stairs. Hurry!" he whispered.

Frantically Casey jammed the last key in the lock and turned it. She twisted the knob in her hand and the door opened. They tiptoed into the room and ran as quietly as they could to the closet in the back.

Hearts pounding, they crouched on the closet floor.

"You think you're so smart, Casey," Walter whispered furiously. "Think Leo is such a dope. Well, he's not so dumb after all."

"Ssh," she said. "He'll probably be gone in a minute. I see him at the park every Saturday playing tennis with some old geezer. He'll probably be gone in a minute."

For a long time they sat there. Then Casey poked her head out of the closet to listen. "Probably gone already." She tiptoed to the side of the classroom and peered out the window. "See? There he goes. I told you, Walt. Easy as pie."

"Some pie," he muttered.

She skipped over to Van's desk. "Just look at this stuff, neat as anything." She pulled out a stack of papers carefully clipped together. "Yup. Right here. Class list. We'll just take this along to the ditto room and shove the rest of the stuff back.

Walter sighed and followed her downstairs to the ditto room. "You still haven't told me—"

"Well, it just so happens that in this envelope I've been carrying around is a ditto master I wrote last night. It's supposed to be part of the class newspaper."

"What do you mean, supposed to be?"

"I'm going to run off a few copies. One or two. Then I'm going to give Tracy a little treat in her next letter."

"Tracy Matson?"

"Listen, Walter, are you supposed to be some kind of an echo? You sound like a parrot. I'm trying to explain to you. Tracy will flip when she sees this copy of *The Ogden School Observer*. She'll really think she has a celebrity for a pen pal."

88

Casey poked her head out of the closet.

When they reached the ditto room, Casey clipped the ditto master to the machine and pressed the button. She watched with satisfaction as the copies started to flip out of the end of the machine into a catcher, looking neat, professional, and smelling deliciously of ditto ink. She shut off the machine and held up a copy.

Suddenly Walter yelled. "Here comes Leo again. Let's get out of here."

Hastily she grabbed up the rest of the copies and raced back to the office to return Mrs. Fiedler's keys. Then she followed Walter downstairs into the cafeteria and out the window. It wasn't until they reached the schoolyard that she began to feel uneasy. Had she forgotten something? She stood there for a moment thinking. Then she shrugged and pounded out of the schoolyard gate.

18

Dear Tracy,

   I'm enclosing a story that will be run in *The Ogden School Observer* this week. I know you'll be glad to hear I escaped without injury.

CASEY VALENTINE RECEIVES MEDALS FOR SAVING THE OGDEN SCHOOL FROM TREMENDOUS FIRE

The principal, Mr. Rosenstrauss, explained to the press that there was complete panic when the Ogden School furnace blew up. People ran for their lives. Mrs. Petty tried to put the fire out by spraying water through her teeth.

   Casey Valentine, however, showed great courage. She carried Mrs. Petty out on her back, led the children to safety, and returned, battling smoke and fire, to grab Mrs. Crump, who was running off dittos that said, "School closed for five years because of fire."

The President of the United States made a special stop at the school to present Casey Valentine with a medal. "This young lady is really a celebrity," the President said. "When the school is rebuilt, the town should name it after this heroine."

The President also told the crowd that the President of France has invited Casey for a trip to Paris to receive the Croix de Guerre for bravery. (And also because she knows French.)

You'll be happy to know, Tracy, that instead of naming the new school for me, I suggested they call it the Walter Moles School for our dear old friend.

Love,
Cassandra Eleanor

19

Casey banged the back door shut, dropped a bag of chance stubs and money on the table, and collapsed on a kitchen chair. Van turned from the counter where she was pouring herself a glass of soda. "Where have you been all day? Mom's having a fit. It's almost suppertime and you haven't even had your lunch yet."

"Selling chances for the newspaper." Casey dug into the bag. "I took your class list out of your desk this morning. Better take it back before I lose it or something. Things like that have a way of happening to me."

"How did you get into the school? Are you crazy, going in there on a Saturday?"

"That was ages ago, early this morning. Worked out perfectly fine, *très amusant*." She shrugged out of her jacket. "How about pouring me a little of that soda instead of taking the whole bottle like a big hog?"

"I went to the store for it," Van answered mildly as she took a tall yellow glass out of the cabinet.

"Sorry," Casey said, feeling guilty. She smiled. "You should see how much money I collected, Vanny. I sold chances to half the fourth-graders and got to twenty of the twenty-three kids in your class."

"What happened to the other three?"

"Two weren't home and the third kid kept saying he didn't speak any English."

"That's Gordie Haywell. He does that to be smart."

"Sounds like an idiot, just like Goony Reed."

"Goony's not such an idiot," Van said.

Casey wiped her mouth with the back of her hand. "You must be joking. All Goony does is pester me, tease—"

"You mean like last night?"

"Exactly. Who'd want to dig up my private property in the middle of the night unless he was a complete dummy like Gunther?" She ran her tongue over her braces.

"Sometimes you're really blind, Casey," Van answered. "About yourself and everybody else."

"I can see enough to know that Goony's a pain in the A."

"That's because he likes you and doesn't know how to act."

Casey brushed her bangs off her forehead. "Likes me? That's what his mother said when I was at his house."

She picked up the bag of money and dumped it out on the table. "Likes me," she muttered to herself. "I

94

never even thought of that. And his father probably killed him last night when he got home."

She started to count. "Over a dollar. Add that to the money the other kids will collect, and the newspaper money when we sell the paper, and we'll probably have the biggest treasury in the school."

Van swallowed the last of her soda. "You're really something. We have about forty cents in the sixth-grade treasury."

"Don't tell me I've finally done something better than Van Valentine, smartest girl in the school?"

"Is that what you think?" Van laughed. "The only reason I get such good marks is because I spend so much time studying. Practically anyone can do that."

Casey grunted. "That's what you think. And how about being such a great gymnast?"

Van leaned over and touched her toes. "Nothing to it, old girl. Everybody's good at something."

Casey clicked her teeth. "I just wish I knew what I'm good at."

They both jumped as the kitchen door banged open. Mr. Valentine stood there, juggling a roller and two cans of paint.

"This should finish up the hall," he said. He put the roller on the counter and the paint cans on the floor. "Your room is next, girls," he said. "And I hope it's the last time I have to cover up fingerprints all over the ceiling."

"I'll wash my hands before I practice from now on," Van promised. "But we still haven't decided on a color yet. Maybe dusty rose instead of blue."

"Yucky," Casey said. She stared out the window

dreamily. "If you don't want the Olympic colors, how about a nice plum color? Maybe just on two walls and the ceiling—with a light green on the third wall and—"

"That's not a paint job, that's a nightmare." Van giggled.

Casey glared at her and stood up briskly. "I have no time to worry about this painting business now, anyway. I've got to go upstairs and think about writing my article for the newspaper. It was supposed to be finished yesterday."

She blew a kiss to her father and raced up the stairs to her bedroom.

20

Casey pretended she was reading her social studies book with the rest of the class until it looked as if Mrs. Petty were falling asleep in front of the room. Then she pulled out her article. It still wasn't finished. She was late as usual; it was a good thing Goony had brought his father's typewriter to school so he could type at the last minute.

She hadn't been able to decide on something to write all weekend. By the time she had remembered to tell Walter that they were supposed to do something with weather observations, it was too late to start.

In desperation, just before bedtime Sunday night, she had glanced at the barometer her father had given her for her birthday, and decided to do an article about it. But even though it was a handy little gadget for her science experiments with Walter, writing about it was pretty dull.

She looked in the encyclopedia, changed some words around in her mind, and began to write. But halfway through the article, she had yawned and decided to finish it in the classroom Monday morning.

Now she read it over and quickly added two last sentences. Then she sat back to think about the newspaper that was coming out at lunchtime. Mrs. Petty had promised that the class could have the drawing for the prize at eleven o'clock and that the committee could go downstairs and run the paper off in the ditto room right after that. But it seemed as if the clock weren't moving at all.

She glanced over toward Gunther in the seat next to hers. She wondered if Van was right. Maybe Goony actually . . . Just then he looked up and noticed her staring at him. She smiled tentatively. In reply, he made a horrible face.

He pulled a folded piece of paper out of the back of his social studies book and tossed it on her desk. "How's this article by the roving reporter?" he whispered.

Casey glanced up at Mrs. Petty, but she was still sitting in front of the room, head bowed over the social studies book. Quietly Casey unfolded the paper. In large block letters Gunther had written across the page:

BEADS FROM BANGKOK BURIED FOREVER

Angrily she started to make a face but noticed he was grinning.

Suddenly she began to laugh.

"Did you get into much trouble the other night?" she whispered.

He shook his head. "Nah, no more than usual."

She picked up the paper. "You're not really going to—"

He grinned again. "Nah. I guess not."

Mrs. Petty looked up over her glasses. "Cassandra, will you read the last paragraph, please?"

Casey jumped. She ran her finger down the page to find the place. In a loud voice she read about the prairie and the building of the sod houses. At last, with relief, she closed the book with a bang.

Mrs. Petty looked at her watch. "It's time now to have our raffle. We'll choose the winner so the committee can print the name in this afternoon's newspaper." She looked around at the class. "I think it would be fitting for our editor to draw the name out of the box. Cassandra, will you come up here?"

"*Naturellement*," said Casey, delighted, and sailed up to the front of the room.

Mrs. Petty shook the box of chances and held it over Casey's head. Standing on tiptoe, Casey reached into the box and dug around to get to the very bottom, then pulled out a folded piece of paper.

"Who is it? Who won?" Joanne yelled.

Mrs. Petty smiled. "I guess you'll have to buy a copy of the paper to find out. Only the committee will know before the paper is distributed this afternoon." She turned to Casey. "You and the rest of the committee may put your things away now and go down to the ditto room."

Hastily Casey slid her social studies book into her desk and followed Darlene and Mindy out to the hall. Gunther trailed behind them, lugging the heavy typewriter. As soon as the classroom door closed behind them, Darlene and Mindy stopped in the middle of the hall. "Who won?" they whispered together.

Casey fished around in her pocket and pulled out the slip of paper. She unfolded it, looked down at the careful writing, and gulped. "It says," she announced, "Edith M. Petty."

"Good grief," Darlene said.

Gunther set the typewriter on the floor and waved his hand to get the circulation going again. "How did her name get in there?"

"I sold her a ticket," Casey admitted. "A nickel is a nickel. Besides, I never thought she'd win."

"I bet half the school will be mad as anything when they find out a teacher won the prize—" Mindy began.

"And blame it on the editor," Casey added glumly.

"It was a crummy prize, anyway," Darlene said.

Casey glanced at Mindy quickly. "My mother thinks it's a very good game," she said and pretended not to notice Mindy's grateful look. "Let's go, everybody, or the paper won't even be out this afternoon."

Downstairs she rattled the knob of the ditto room door. "Locked. Wait here and I'll get the key." She hurried down the hall to the office.

Mrs. Crump, the secretary, sat at her desk, typing.

Casey stood there waiting. When Mrs. Crump didn't look up, she said, "Excuse me, the ditto room is . . ."

The secretary looked up briefly, her severe brown

eyes magnified by thick, round glasses, "I'm busy. You'll have to wait."

The second hand swept around the large office clock as Casey stood there, fidgeting from one foot to the other. It was ten minutes after eleven and Gunther still had to type her article. They'd never be ready to set up their stand in front of the cafeteria by lunchtime.

Finally Mrs. Crump looked up again. "What is it, Van?" she asked irritably.

"Casey." She landed on one foot. "I'm Casey."

"Well, what do you want?"

"We're supposed to run something off on the ditto machine, but the door's locked."

Mrs. Crump scraped back her chair and scooped up a ring of keys from the corner of her desk. "Have to do everything around here," she complained as she clicked down the hall ahead of Casey. "Attendance cards to be typed, telephones ringing constantly. Now I have to be the custodian too." She twisted the key in the lock and swung the door open. "Hurry up, children. In a little while I have to use the ditto machine for an important memo for Mr. Rosenstrauss." She turned and hurried back to the office.

"Hurry, Goony," Casey said and held the door open for him.

He heaved the typewriter up on a table and flipped in a ditto master. "Give me your article," he said.

She handed him her paper, feeling a little uncomfortable. Now that she thought about it, her article really wasn't good at all.

Gunther looked at the title, "Important Facts About

"Hurry up, children," Mrs. Crump said.

Barometers." "Hmm," he said. "This seems like a really interesting and informative article."

She giggled. "Best I could think of. You know, Goony, I'm just realizing, I'm not the best writer in the world."

He looked up. "Well, you organized the whole paper. That's something, isn't it?"

She looked over his shoulder for a moment while he typed. He really wasn't the best typist in the world either, she noticed. Twice he ripped the ditto master out of the machine, crumpled the paper into a ball, and threw it on the floor.

It wasn't until eleven thirty that he typed the last sentence. At the same time, there was a click at the door. Mrs. Crump's face peered around the edge. "Are you still here? Not finished? What have you children been doing all this time?"

"We're going to run off—" Casey said.

"Too late," Mrs. Crump interrupted. "Much too late. Mr. Rosenstrauss needs his memo dittoed up right away."

"But—" Casey began.

"No buts, Van," Mrs. Crump said emphatically. "Leave your ditto masters here. If I have the time I'll run them off for you. But I doubt it very much. Go back to your classroom, and I'll send for you when they're finished."

21

There was nothing they could do but leave the ditto room. Slowly they trailed up the stairs to the classroom.

"Forty-eight posters all over this building," Casey moaned. "Every kid in the school expecting to read our newspaper at lunchtime." She shook her head. "What an old creep she is." She shoved the classroom door open.

Mrs. Petty looked at them inquiringly.

"Mrs. Crump wanted to use the ditto machine," Casey said. She watched Mrs. Petty for a moment, hoping that she might think of a way to help them.

But Mrs. Petty just shrugged. "Too bad," she said before she turned back to the blackboard.

Might have known, Casey told herself, and slammed into her seat. She slapped her notebook on the desk and began to copy her work.

By the time the clock said two minutes to twelve, she had finished most of the fill-in-the-blanks Mrs. Petty had chalked on the board. She was fishing around in her desk for her lunch bag when the door opened. Mrs. Crump stood there, lips pressed together, a pile of paper in her outstretched hands.

Casey looked at her. She couldn't believe it. It looked as if the old creep had done the newspaper for them. She watched as Mrs. Petty motioned to Joanne in the first seat to take the papers.

Mrs. Crump glared at them through her thick, round glasses. "I have the newspaper. Three pages, run off, stapled, ready to go."

Darlene looked over at Casey and held up three fingers. "Three?" she whispered. "What's she talking about?"

Casey circled her ear with her index finger. "Flipped," she mouthed. The old idiot's gone crazy, she thought to herself—the newspaper was only two pages.

"I don't know what those children were doing down there. Fooling around. Nonsense and silliness. They should have mentioned that they had already clipped one page of the paper into the ditto machine."

Casey spoke up. "We did not."

"Are you calling me a liar, young lady? Your name was right on the top of the page." Mrs. Crump turned to Mrs. Petty. "There was no sense in my taking their page out to start Mr. Rosenstrauss's work. Waste of effort. So I ran theirs off first."

Casey brushed away an uneasy feeling as she listened to Mrs. Petty thank Mrs. Crump. "I'm sure," said

Mrs. Petty, "the children are very grateful." She looked at Casey.

Darlene and Casey spoke together. "Thank you, Mrs. Crump."

As the secretary marched out of the room, Mrs. Petty tapped her hand on the desk. "Hurry," she said to the committee. "You'll have time to set your newspaper up on the table outside the cafeteria before the rest of the school comes in for lunch."

Casey tugged her lunch bag out of her desk and sped to the front of the room. She scooped up the news-papers and led the way down to the first floor.

To one side of the large double doors in front of the cafeteria was a long metal table. Together they arranged the newspapers in neat rows, glancing down at the top sheet. *The Ogden School Observer*, typed across the top, made the paper look professional, and their articles typed by Gunther with only a few cross-outs didn't look bad either.

In the center of the first page was a large box, which read:

MRS. EDITH M. PETTY

WINS PRIZE

Casey ran her finger across it. "A shame," she said. "Teachers have to get into everything around here."

Darlene took a box out of her lunch bag and held it up. "To collect our money," she said.

Casey nodded.

"Hey, Casey," Mindy asked, "what do you think Mrs. Crump meant about three pages instead of two?"

Casey started to flip to the third page, but a class marched down the stairs and across the hall toward the cafeteria doors. The front of the line stopped when the children saw the newspapers. Within a few minutes clumps of children surrounded the table, holding out money, and by the time the last class had filed by them, Darlene's cash box was full.

With five minutes left of the lunch hour, every copy was sold except for the four Casey had tucked under the table for the committee. She pulled them out and stretched. "I guess that's it, kids," she said. "Time for us to have a quick lunch."

They went through the double doors into the cafeteria just as three sixth-grade girls were coming out. They looked at her curiously. One said, "You're Casey Valentine, right?"

Casey nodded with satisfaction. Not Van's sister. Herself. Casey. They knew exactly who she was. She turned to look after them and was surprised to find that they had turned to look at her. But they were giggling.

Puzzled, Casey headed for the fourth-grade tables with Darlene and Mindy. The rest of the class had finished lunch and were in the schoolyard until the bell rang.

"I can't wait to read this over, can you?" Mindy asked them through a mouth filled with peanut butter.

Darlene nodded. "Nice of Mrs. Crump to get it ready for us. I wonder why she thought there were three pages, though, when there were only two?"

Casey flipped the newspaper open. "There are

three," she began in a surprised voice. "Look. One, two . . ." and gasped.

Almost jumping out at her on the third page were the large block letters she had printed so carefully for Tracy Matson's letter:

CASEY VALENTINE RECEIVES MEDALS FOR SAVING THE OGDEN SCHOOL FROM TREMENDOUS FIRE

22

Suddenly it was clear to her. She knew exactly what had happened. On Saturday when Leo had come back to the school, she had grabbed up the copies she'd made for Tracy's letter but had completely forgotten the ditto master still in the machine. Mrs. Crump must have thought it was part of their paper and had run it off and stapled it right to *The Ogden School Observer*.

She stared at the newspaper. Finally she folded the paper in half, stuck it in her pocket, and swung her legs over the bench. "I've got to go to the girls' room, kids," she said in a strangled voice.

Mindy looked up from her milk. "You'd better hurry. The bell is going to ring in a few minutes and I haven't even had time to read our paper."

Casey scurried out of the cafeteria and down the hall to the girls' room. Inside, she glanced in the mirror.

Her freckles stood out like big brown blotches against her long white face, and her bangs, as usual, hung down over her eyes. She looked terrible. Maybe she could go upstairs to Mrs. Petty and tell her that she was sick—flu maybe, or a virus—and that she'd better go home right away.

Too bad it wouldn't work. She might be able to fool Mrs. Petty about being sick, but she'd never fool her mother. Mom would have her back in school in five minutes.

She banged open one of the gray metal toilet doors and bolted it behind her. Instead of spreading paper on the seat the way her mother always told her to, she sat down and took the newspaper out of her pocket. Smoothing it out on her lap, she read it carefully.

It was every bit as bad as she had expected. In fact, it was worse. The only way she could ever get out of the mess she was in was to hope that the school furnace would explode in the next two minutes and that she could personally rescue twenty-five people before the whole school read the paper. Even then she wasn't too sure that the President of the United States could be expected to be sitting around waiting to present her with a medal for bravery.

What she looked like, she thought bitterly, was a kid who wanted to be important and didn't have one thing to be important about. She caught her lip between her teeth. It was the truth. And the rest of the truth was that she was jealous of Van.

She heard the outside door of the girls' room open and peered out through the space between the door and the frame. It was Sue Verona and two other girls in the sixth grade.

She listened, face burning, as Sue asked the other girls, "Did you read the newspaper the fourth-graders did?"

One of the girls said, "Mrs. Petty won the prize."

"It wasn't such a hot prize anyway," someone said.

At that moment the bell rang. Lunch hour was over. Casey leaned forward to hear what Sue Verona was saying as the three girls slammed out of the girls' room, laughing. She thought she'd heard something about a fire.

Casey covered her face with her hands and stayed in the booth a few minutes longer. Finally she left it and took awhile to wash her hands.

By this time, she thought, everyone would be back in their classrooms. She was right. There wasn't a soul in the hall when she came out of the girls' room. She trudged upstairs to her room. Mrs. Petty was saying, "Now that's enough talk about the newspaper. Back to work." Casey slid into her seat.

For the rest of the afternoon she sat there, hardly raising her head even when Mrs. Petty complimented the committee on a job well done.

When dismissal time came at last, Casey grabbed her sweater off the hook in the closet and hurried to the front of the line. She broke into a run as Mrs. Petty dismissed the line at the schoolyard gate, and she never stopped, even though she could hear Walter pounding after her, yelling for her to wait up.

She raced up the driveway to the Secret Passageway,

threw her books over in front of her, and climbed the fence. Out of breath, she sank down and leaned against a rock in the center of the Passageway. She tried to ignore Walter, who was coming up the driveway, still yelling for her.

He clambered over the fence and landed next to her. "Go away, will you, Walt? I need to be alone for a while."

"The Great Valentine alone? Just when you're finally a celebrity?" he asked.

"Don't be funny," she said sourly. "Everyone must think I'm some kind of an idiot."

"Why?" He started to laugh. "How did you ever think that up about carrying Mrs. Petty out on your back?"

She covered her face with her hands. "Don't talk about it. Don't say one more word. I've got to get out of here. Run away or something. If this were the old days I could skip out as a stowaway on a boat."

"Hang around doing crazy things, maybe you could be sent to reform school instead. That would get you out of here all right." He cocked his head. "Is that your mother calling you?"

She ran her tongue over her braces. "Yeah. There's no peace in the whole world." She picked up her books and stood up. "If I ever get another idea, just remind me of this awful mess."

He looked up at her, the sun glinting on his glasses. "You'll get another idea by tomorrow—or the next day at the latest." He laughed. "Don't worry, kid. Someday you'll make a million dollars with your ideas."

Casey climbed the fence. Waving halfheartedly at Walter over her shoulder, she walked up the driveway to her house.

Through the kitchen window she could see Van and her mother sitting at the table. She ducked when she saw her mother reading Van's copy of *The Ogden School Observer*. Why did Van have to go and show her mother that? She could feel tears burning her eyes.

In the kitchen her mother began to laugh. "Wonderful," she said.

"That Casey is really something," Van said. "The rest of the paper was pretty dull. But everybody thought Casey's letter was terrific. Even Mrs. Petty liked it. She stopped me on the way out and said that she wanted me to give the Standout game to Casey. She said she deserved it for being so creative."

"It's true," her mother answered. "She certainly is."

Casey stood outside on one foot. She couldn't believe it. "Creative." They all thought she had written the letter on purpose. To be funny. And Van had sounded so proud of her!

She opened the kitchen door and put her books on the table. Grinning shyly at her mother and Van, she said slowly, "I was thinking—maybe we could paint our room dusty pink, after all."

"You can do better than that." Van laughed. "How about midnight black?"

Casey squinted at the ceiling, considering. "Not bad. We could add a few touches of hot pink."

Her mother tapped *The Ogden School Observer* lightly. "Whatever you decide, Casey, I'm sure it will be original."

Casey nodded, smiling. "Listen," she said. "I've got to call Darlene. Ask her to come over. Mindy too." She picked up her books and started for the telephone. It was about time they all learned how to play Standout.

And tonight, when she had some time, she had a letter to write. It was about time she did something about Tracy Matson too.

23

Dear Tracy,

I received your letter the other day. I was happy to hear from you. There are some things I have to tell you.

First. I really am a celebrity. There's no doubt about that. Not only does everybody know my name now but I can't even go to the bathroom in school without hearing people talking about me.

But:

1. I'm not rich, just regular.
2. I know only about twenty words in French.
3. Walter is not dead anymore.
4. I just found out that my sister is not nearly the weasel I thought she was. In fact, she may turn out to be a celebrity herself, with a little help.

Love,
Casey

"Dear Tracy, I really am a celebrity."

P.S. Do you remember that horrible, icky, disgusting boy, Gunther Reed, I told you about? I just noticed that he's the best-looking boy in the class. (After Walter, of course.) In fact, he'll be a lot of fun when he stops trying to impress everybody in the whole world.